HOPSCOTCH

Bear
in Town

18

D1188073

2644181

First published in 2004 by
Franklin Watts
96 Leonard Street
London
EC2A 4XD

Franklin Watts Australia
45–51 Huntley Street
Alexandria
NSW 2015

A CIP catalogue record for this book is available
from the British Library.

ISBN 0 7496 5871 1 (hbk)
ISBN 0 7496 5875 4 (pbk)

Series Editor: Jackie Hamley
Series Advisor: Dr Barrie Wade
Cover Design: Jason Anscomb
Design: Peter Scoulding

Printed in China

For Mum, Dad and Rebecca – R.W.

HOPSCOTCH

Bear in Town

by A. H. Benjamin and Richard Watson

W
FRANKLIN WATTS
LONDON•SYDNEY

Once there was a bear who lived
at the edge of the forest.

Not far away, the bear could
see a town. "I'd love to go
there," he thought to himself.
"But bears aren't allowed
in towns."

Then, one morning, the bear had an idea: "I'll wear a disguise!"

That afternoon, the bear dressed up as a window cleaner and walked into town. Nobody noticed anything unusual about him.

A shopkeeper asked him to
clean her windows.

"Look at that window cleaner!"
the people laughed. "He's not
using a sponge!"

"Oops!" thought the bear, realising his mistake. He ran away to hide.

Next, the bear tried to be a beekeeper. He kept lots of bees and collected lots of honey.

Then he took the honey into town to sell.

But the bear found the honey a
bit too tasty to sell!
"Why are you eating all the honey?"
asked the customers, angrily.

"Gulp!" said the bear as he
swallowed the last drop.
Again he ran away to hide.

Then the bear tried to be a jogger.
He put on a pink tracksuit and
trotted into the park.

He saw two joggers ahead and wanted to catch up with them.

"How come you can run on four legs?" asked the joggers in surprise.

"Oh no!" thought the bear, and
he jogged away to hide.

Next, the bear tried to be a
firefighter. He looked very
smart in his uniform.
The bear saw a cat
stuck up a tree.

He rescued the cat in no time.
"Only a bear could climb a tree so
quickly!" said the crowd, amazed.

"Not again!" thought the bear as he
handed the cat back to her owner.

The bear went back to the forest. "Grrrr," he thought, "it's not so easy to fool people. But there must be a way for me to get into town!"

Then he had a brilliant idea!

The bear went into town again.

This time he wore nothing at all.

In the street, he rolled on the ground.

He scratched his back against the cars and roared loudly.

But the people just laughed.
"Look at that man in a
bear suit!" they cried.
"At last!" thought
the bear.

Hopscotch has been specially designed to fit the requirements of the National Literacy Strategy. It offers real books by top authors and illustrators for children developing their reading skills.

There are 25 Hopscotch stories to choose from:

Marvin, the Blue Pig
Written by Karen Wallace
Illustrated by Lisa Williams

Plip and Plop
Written by Penny Dolan
Illustrated by Lisa Smith

The Queen's Dragon
Written by Anne Cassidy
Illustrated by Gwyneth Williamson

Flora McQuack
Written by Penny Dolan
Illustrated by Kay Widdowson

Willie the Whale
Written by Joy Oades
Illustrated by Barbara Vagnozzi

Naughty Nancy
Written by Anne Cassidy
Illustrated by Desideria Guicciardini

Run!
Written by Sue Ferraby
Illustrated by Fabiano Fiorin

The Playground Snake
Written by Brian Moses
Illustrated by David Mostyn

"Sausages!"
Written by Anne Adeney
Illustrated by Roger Fereday

The Truth about Hansel and Gretel
Written by Karina Law
Illustrated by Elke Counsell

Pippin's Big Jump
Written by Hilary Robinson
Illustrated by Sarah Warburton

Whose Birthday Is It?
Written by Sherryl Clark
Illustrated by Jan Smith

The Princess and the Frog
Written by Margaret Nash
Illustrated by Martin Remphry

Flynn Flies High
Written by Hilary Robinson
Illustrated by Tim Archbold

Clever Cat
Written by Karen Wallace
Illustrated by Anni Axworthy

Moo!
Written by Penny Dolan
Illustrated by Melanie Sharp

Izzie's Idea
Written by Jillian Powell
Illustrated by Leonie Shearing

Roly-poly Rice Ball
Written by Penny Dolan
Illustrated by Diana Mayo

I Can't Stand It!
Written by Anne Adeney
Illustrated by Mike Phillips

Cockerel's Big Egg
Written by Damian Harvey
Illustrated by François Hall

The Truth about those Billy Goats
Written by Karina Law
Illustrated by Graham Philpot

Bear in Town
Written by A. H. Benjamin
Illustrated by Richard Watson

Marlowe's Mum and the Tree House
Written by Karina Law
Illustrated by Ross Collins

The Best Den Ever
Written by Anne Cassidy
Illustrated by Deborah Allwright

How to Teach a Dragon Manners
Written by Hilary Robinson
Illustrated by Jane Abbott